AMERICAN BEGINNINGS

You're Right There!

by Alan Kramer
illustrated by Richard Kolding

Cast of Characters

Newscaster

Reporters

American Citizens

British Soldiers and Officers

John Adams

King George

King George's Advisers

Paul Revere

Sam Adams

The Tea Singers

George Washington

Benjamin Franklin

Betsy Ross

Thomas Jefferson

Delegates to the Continental Congress

NOTE: You will often see
"Thank you, [reporter's name]." That means you
should add the name of the reporter, such as:
"Thank you, Mary."

Setting

American Beginnings takes place between March 5, 1770, and July 4, 1776. It takes us through many of the most important events in the history of American independence—the Boston Massacre, the Boston Tea Party, the design of the first American flag, the British attack on Lexington and Concord, and the signing of the Declaration of Independence.

Some Suggestions for Staging

The play can be staged with many players or with just a few. For example, the eight major historical figures could be played by eight actors or by fewer, each playing more than one part. The American Citizens, British Soldiers, King's Advisers, and Delegates can also be played by as few as two actors dividing each set of parts, or by many actors, each taking an individual part.

Costumes, Sets, and Props

American Beginnings doesn't require elaborate costumes or sets. For example, an open space for the Concord green or lines of desks for the Continental Congress should be enough. Simple "colonial" costumes (long pants pulled up to the knee, white shirts, and jackets) and a few simple props (an American flag, muskets, barrels or boxes for tea, etc.) will also work well. The play may be done continuously or scene by scene.

Scene 1

Newscaster: Hello and welcome to *You're Right There!*, WBEC's new TV series, which takes you right to where history is being made. It's . . . *(checking a clock)* . . . March 5, 1770, and we take you to the British colony in North America. The people who live here call it America. As you may know, they've been having some trouble with the King of England over taxes. For more on this, we take you to Boston, Massachusetts, and our at-the-time reporter, [Reporter A's name].

Reporter A: *(holding a microphone)* Thank you, [Newscaster's name]. The British troops have set up camp here on the Boston Common, and the people of Boston are not happy about it—I can tell you that! Here come some citizens now. Hello, Citizens.

Citizen: You mean us?

4

Reporter A: *(holding out a microphone)* Yes. What do you think about the British soldiers being here?

Citizen: *(looking "strangely" at the microphone but answering anyway)* Well, I think it's a disgrace. A disgrace!

Citizen: We're Americans. We're not British any longer! *(Other Citizens agree.)*

Citizen: Since we don't have the rights that British citizens get, why should we pay their taxes? *(Other Citizens agree.)*

Citizen: They don't ask us what we want, but they're sure quick to send soldiers to keep us quiet. *(Other Citizens agree.)*

Citizen: A disgrace! That's what it is. *(Other Citizens agree.)*

Citizen: *(to the crowd)* No taxation without representation! *(loud cheer from the crowd)*

Reporter A: Thank you. *(British soldiers come over.)* Sir? Officer? British soldier? Hello??

British Soldier: What is it?

Reporter A: Americans are saying . . .

British Soldier: I heard what they said. But why do you call them "Americans"? *(He says this with distaste.)* They're British citizens, just like I am, and they should be loyal to the King, whether they like him or not.

Reporter A: Well, *they* think . . .

British Soldier: *They* think? Who cares what *they* think?? I'm a loyal British subject. I *never* think for myself. Why should "Americans" get to think, when we British don't? *(cheer from the other British soldiers and boos from the American Citizens)*

Reporter A: But it's *important* what the people say.

British Soldier: No it's not! Who cares what the *people* say? In Britain we only listen to what the King says! The people, no. The King, yes.

Reporter A: But isn't it true . . . ?

British Soldier: If the King says something is true, then it's true.

Reporter A: *(angrily)* Hey! Will you stop interrupting already!?!

British Soldier: I'm sorry. That was rude. *(in a proper tone)* A British soldier should never be rude.

Citizen: You don't think it's *rude* to seize our property without asking?

Citizen: You don't think it's *rude* to take over Boston Common for your soldiers?

Citizen: Don't you think it was *rude* to deprive us of our rights?

Citizen: Don't you think it was *rude* to close Boston Harbor to our ships?

British Soldier: If you have complaints, you can write a letter to Parliament. *(The British laugh.)*

Reporter A: *(to the audience)* Well, that sounded pretty rude to me. *(Suddenly, the sound of gunshots is heard. The British Officer grabs his rifle and runs off.)* What was that??

Citizen: *(running onto the stage)* Those are gunshots! The British are shooting!

Reporter A: What happened?

Citizen: Some people were yelling at the British soldiers to go home. A few children started throwing snowballs. Then, all of a sudden, the British started shooting.

Reporter A: *(to the audience)* Let's try to find out if anyone was hurt. Ah—here's John Adams. Maybe he can help us. *(Adams is busily trying to organize people.)* He's a leader of the Sons of Liberty here in Boston. Mr. Adams? Mr. Adams?

John Adams: What is it? I'm very busy right now.

Reporter A: I know, sir, but our audience wants to know what happened.

John Adams: The British started firing. That's all we know for sure.

Citizen: *(running on, approaching Adams)* Mr. Adams. We have word.

John Adams: Yes? What is it?

Citizen: Five have been killed—five citizens of Boston.

John Adams: Oh no!

Citizen: One of them is Crispus Attucks, a freedman—a former slave—and a sailor.

John Adams: Crispus Attucks is a member of the Sons of Liberty. I know him.

Citizen: Kill the British! *(cheers of agreement)*

Citizen: Let's get our own guns and shoot them down! *(more cheers; Citizens start to move off for their guns)*

John Adams: No! *(They all stop.)*

Citizen: But they've shot our citizens. They must be punished!

John Adams: And they will be. But by the law. Not by the guns of a mob.

Citizen: But they used their guns to kill us.

John Adams: And they will be punished for that. But we Americans believe in justice, even if the British do not. I'm a lawyer, and I will defend the British soldiers, even though I hate everything they're doing here. Come, my fellow citizens, let us discuss this together. *(Adams leads the others off in discussion.)*

Reporter A: Well, there you have it. For the first time, British soldiers have killed American citizens. This could mean war! Now back to [Newscaster's name] in our studios.

Scene 2

Newscaster: Thank you, [Reporter A]. That's all from Boston. It appears that King George has asked to give his side of the story. We now take you to WBEC's at-the-time reporter in London, England. Take it away, [Reporter B's name].

Reporter B: Thank you, [Newscaster's name]. All right, Mr. King. What do you have to say?

King George: *(sitting on his throne [chair])* Your Highness.

Reporter B: What?

King George: The proper term is "Your Highness."

Reporter B: *Whatever.* Go ahead.

King George: *(talking to his adviser)* What do I do?

Adviser: Look this way and start talking. *(The Adviser turns the King to face the audience.)*

King George: All right. (*He stands up straight.*) I am King George III. Your King. The only King you are going to have. Everyone must have a King, and I'm your King. Thank you very much. (*He goes to sit down.*)

Adviser: Your Highness.

King George: What?

Adviser: (*prompting*) "The Americans . . ."

King George: Ah, yes. You people who call yourselves Americans, you've been saying some not-very-nice things about me, now haven't you? (*He wags a finger but doesn't say anything.*)

Reporter B: Like what?

Adviser: Well, a lot of them think that he's a tyrant.

King George: What? (*He looks like he wants to hit his Adviser.*)

Adviser: I only meant that that's what *they* say you are. I think you're very nice.

King George: Oh.

Reporter B: What else?

Adviser: They say that he doesn't care about their problems.

Adviser: That he's mean.

Adviser: And arrogant! *(They're starting to get into this now.)*

Adviser: And bossy—they call him *that* all the time! And—

King George: Stop it!! *(The Advisers stop.)* Who cares what they say? They're wrong. I'm right. I'm the King, and they're not. That's all I have to say. The end.

Reporter B: So you can raise taxes any time you want to? You don't have to ask anybody?

King George: *Ask* someone?? Who's the King around here, you or me?

Reporter B: And the Stamp Acts and Townshend Acts and all those other things that you had Parliament impose on the colonies . . .?

King George: Complain, complain, complain. That's all these *Americans* do. What do they think this is? A democracy? *(They laugh.)* Well, that's all I have to say. This is your King saying good-bye. And remember: Pay those taxes!

Reporter B: *(back to the audience)* So you heard it here first. King George III says . . . *(The Adviser talks loudly, congratulating the King. The Reporter can't talk over the noise.)*

Adviser: Brilliant! That part about this not being a democracy! *(They laugh.)*

Adviser: *(quoting King George)* "Complain, complain, complain." *(They laugh some more.)*

Newscaster: *(The Newscaster points his remote. The Adviser and the King keep talking but no sound comes out. He takes out his watch and reads.)* We now fast-forward to December 16, 1773. *(The Newscaster points the remote and pushes the fast-forward button. King George and his Advisers fast-forward offstage as Reporter C and others fast-forward on.)* [Reporter C's name] is standing by in Boston Harbor, where some sort of activity is taking place.

Scene 3

Reporter C: Thank you, [Newscaster's name]. As you can see, I'm standing here by Boston Harbor. There are people here. They look like Native Americans, and they're carrying barrels of tea. Let's see if we can speak with one of them. Sir?

Paul Revere: Yes?

Reporter C: Wait—you're not a Native American!

Paul Revere: No. Actually, my name is Paul Revere. I'm a silversmith. I make the finest silver mugs and bowls in Boston. I also make wooden teeth. (*He opens his mouth.*) See? (*sounding like a commercial*) Come to my modern shop on Beacon Hill in Boston. There you will find . . .

Reporter C: Mr. Revere?

Paul Revere: Sorry.

Reporter C: Can you tell our viewers what you are doing here today?

Paul Revere: You've heard about the tax on tea that King George and his Parliament have tried to impose on us?

Reporter C: Of course.

Paul Revere: We've decided to show the King exactly how much we *don't* like his taxes. *(Sam Adams joins him.)* Here—let Sam Adams explain. He's the head of the Sons of Liberty.

Sam Adams: As long as there are British taxes on this tea, we're not going to let it off the boats. So since they won't take it back to England, we're going to dump it in Boston Harbor. Let the fish drink tea tonight.

Reporter C: You'd rather throw away the tea than pay taxes on it?

Sam Adams: We'd be willing to pay the tax if it were *our* tax, if *we* got to decide about it.

Paul Revere: How about a tax to support the poor people of Boston? Or a tax to fix our roads? Or a tax to help our schools?

Sam Adams: But the King and Parliament want to tax our tea to pay for *their* empire and *their* wars. And that we won't do. That's why my friends and I are going to dump the tea. (*The protesters start dumping barrels of tea over the side of the ship and into the water. They exit, congratulating one another.*)

Scene 4

Newscaster: Well, there it is. All the tea, gone—splash!—into the water. King George isn't going to be happy about this! Let's hear what he has to say.

King George: (*marching onstage with his Advisers*) No, I am not happy at all! (*to the audience*) How dare these Americans take my tea and dump it into the water like that? What's happening in this world when people think they have the right to make up their own rules? (*He marches off, his Advisers following.*)

Newscaster: Well. There you have it. King George is getting angrier by the minute! Stay tuned, viewers, and we'll see what happens next. But before we fast-forward to our next scene, let's take a break for a commercial. We'll be right back.

Scene 5

(The Tea Singers come out. They hold bags of tea as they sing [to the tune for "Twinkle, Twinkle, Little Star"].)

You should really drink our tea,
The best that any tea can be.
It's better than those British brands,
With taxes no one understands.
So be sure to drink our tea,
Sure tastes good, and you'll be free!

(They bow and wave to the audience as they exit.)

Scene 6

Newscaster: Now for a special bulletin. Paul Revere—you remember, the silversmith from Boston?—has just reported that the British have sent seven hundred troops to march on the towns of Lexington and Concord in Massachusetts. Mr. Revere has been riding all night yelling, "The British are coming!" and calling out the Minutemen to defend the towns. A group of patriots has gathered in the square in Lexington to head off the British. We take you there now.

Reporter D: Thank you, [Newscaster's name]. British troops are everywhere. I'm right in the middle of them now. Officer . . .? *(The Reporter holds out the microphone to a British soldier who doesn't stop.) Soldier . . .? (The Reporter tries another soldier.)* Hey, you! *(No one stops.)* This is ridiculous!

(The Newscaster stomps out of the studio and presses the pause button on the remote. All freeze. Then the Newscaster points the remote and pushes the play button. The one officer unfreezes.)

Reporter D: Now, Officer, I have just a few questions.

British Officer: What? *(He looks around at everyone else still frozen.)*

Reporter D: What are you British soldiers doing here?

British Officer: We're marching on Concord. *(He pokes at another soldier, who stays frozen.)* Our spies tell us there are arms and weapons hidden there. How did *you* know we were here? *(A Citizen steps into his path.)*

Citizen: This is *our* country. Anything that happens, we pass the word. Don't look now, but there are three hundred Minutemen on the Concord Bridge waiting for you.

British Officer: Three hundred? Hah! There are seven hundred of us! *(He starts to leave. Another Citizen blocks him.)*

Citizen: Three hundred of us can beat seven hundred of you any day. We're not going to stop fighting until you go back to England.

Citizen: No matter how many of you there are, *we're* going to win because it's *our* country, and we're fighting for *our* homes and families.

British Officer: *(suddenly running off, frightened)* Help!!

Reporter D: Well, I guess we showed *him*! Let's go now to [Newscaster's name]! *(The Newscaster presses the play button. The soldiers unfreeze. Shots are heard.)*

Newscaster: What was that? It sounds like shooting has broken out on the Lexington green!

Newscaster: Come in, [Reporter E]. Can you tell us about some possible shooting in Lexington?

Reporter E: Yes, [Newscaster's name]. We have shooting here on the Lexington green. Eight Minutemen have been killed in the fighting. It looks like our War of Independence has started for real!

Reporter D: And over here, the British troops are now marching toward the Concord Bridge, where American soldiers are standing with their weapons. They're shooting at one another. Wait! The British troops are turning around. They're heading back toward Boston. But the Minutemen are chasing them through the woods. The British are marching in straight rows in their bright red uniforms! Now why are they doing *that*? The Americans are hiding behind trees and shooting at them. You can tell the British have never seen anything like this before. Back to you, [Newscaster's name].

Newscaster: Thank you, Reporters. Now let's fast-forward to June 1775. Come in, [Reporter F's name].

Scene 7

Reporter F: Thank you, [Newscaster's name]. I have someone with me now whom I think everyone would like to meet. It's General George Washington, the new commander in chief.

George Washington: War is a terrible thing. Make sure everyone understands that this is going to be a difficult war. Many will die. But we must fight if we want to be free. *(Benjamin Franklin enters.)* Dr. Franklin! Hello, Ben! It seems our War of Independence has begun.

Benjamin Franklin: Yes. We knew it would, didn't we?

George Washington: We're going to win in the end, aren't we, Ben?

Benjamin Franklin: It's our country, General. We must be independent, or we'll never be free. It will be difficult, but we will win.

George Washington: I hope you're right. Anyway, as I've heard you say, "We must indeed all hang together, or most assuredly, we shall all hang separately."

Benjamin Franklin: That's right. We're rebels now. There's a price on our heads. *(They laugh and start off together.)*

Reporter E: Where are you going?

Benjamin Franklin: I'm going back to Philadelphia. Richard Henry Lee of Virginia has proposed independence to the Second Continental Congress.

George Washington: Finally! We've waited a long time for this moment. What did he say?

Benjamin Franklin: I have it here. *(Franklin unfolds a paper.)* He proposed "that these united colonies are and of right ought to be free and independent states." This will surely make our friend John Adams happy. He's fought for independence all his life. Will you go to Philadelphia, George?

George Washington: No. It is my job to lead the army. We have much to do before we can be a free nation. What about you?

Benjamin Franklin: I wouldn't miss it for anything in the world. They should be reading the Declaration of Independence any time now. Thomas Jefferson has written it, you know.

George Washington: I wish I could be there, Ben. It will be a special moment. *(They exit.)*

Reporter E: *(watching them go)* There go two of the most important leaders of our country. Amazing men. Now we go to our studios in Philadelphia.

Scene 8

Newscaster: We now bring you a special interview with Betsy Ross, a leading patriot, who is creating a flag for the new nation. Ms. Ross, is it true that George Washington himself asked you to make the flag?

Betsy Ross: Yes it is. General Washington and Robert Morris of New Jersey asked me to make it. As you can see, I'm sewing on thirteen red and white stripes, but I'm also adding thirteen stars for the colonies.

Newscaster: Why both stars *and* stripes?

Betsy Ross: The stripes are for our original thirteen colonies, soon to be *states* in a new United States of America. But my hope is that America will keep growing. Each state will have its own star. Can you imagine? Some day we could have twenty or even thirty states!

Newscaster: Wow!

Betsy Ross: That's a lot of sewing to do. I'd better get back to work.

Newscaster: Well, thank you, Ms. Ross, for your time. Would you like to join us for the reading of our Declaration of Independence?

Betsy Ross: Thank you. I'd like that very much.

Scene 9

Newscaster: *(The whole cast comes on stage—some as Delegates and some as regular Citizens—as the scene shifts to Philadelphia.)* Now for the big moment. It's July 4, 1776. We're here at Independence Hall in Philadelphia. We are about to witness an extraordinary event. In just a moment, Thomas Jefferson will be reading from the Declaration of Independence to delegates from all thirteen colonies. Here he is now.

Thomas Jefferson: Honored delegates. As you know, the purpose of this Declaration is to put our cause before the world in language so clear that it commands their understanding and agreement. Mr. Adams, do you have something to add?

John Adams: Thank you, Mr. Jefferson. I just want to remind the delegates that this is only the beginning. We have debated and argued and compromised, but there is more to be done.

Benjamin Franklin: We have not ended slavery, as many of us had wanted. But we will keep working at this until every American is free, no matter what color.

Thomas Jefferson: Or religion.

John Adams: Or background.

Benjamin Franklin: We promise that to all of you.

Thomas Jefferson: And we promise that America will always be free. *(The delegates applaud.)*

Delegate: *(calling out)* Could I read from the Declaration, Mr. Jefferson?

Thomas Jefferson: Why, of course. The Declaration belongs to all of us. *(He hands the Declaration to the Delegate.)* Please read.

Delegate: We hold these truths to be self-evident . . . *(passing the Declaration to the next delegate)*

Delegate: that all men are created equal . . . *(passing it on)*

Delegate: that they are endowed by their Creator with certain unalienable Rights . . . *(and on)*

Delegate: that among these are Life, Liberty, and the pursuit of Happiness. *(and on)*

Scene 10

Newscaster: *(stepping forward among the Citizens as the Delegates continue to read—silently—in the background)* The Declaration of Independence is now official. We will have to fight a war for our independence, but America is now really a nation at last. Let's hear what the people think about that. *(holding out a microphone)* What do you plan to do with your Life, Liberty, and the pursuit of Happiness?

Citizen: I want to be a doctor.

Citizen: I want to be a teacher.

Citizen: I want to be an inventor. I have an idea for a way to use electricity to make light.

Citizen: Electricity?

Citizen: Right. One day Ben Franklin was flying a kite in a rainstorm, and lightning came down the string and made a key light up. He calls it electricity, and he thinks there might be a way to use it in our homes. I want to figure out how!

Newscaster: Good for you.

Citizen: I want to start my own business.

Citizen: In America I can be anything I choose to be. I want to be a rock star.

Newscaster: A rock star? What's a rock star?

Citizen: I don't know, but it sounds cool!

Citizen: I want to have a family. In America, all children can go to school.

Citizen: In America, we can believe in any religion we choose.

Citizen: In America, we can stand up for what we believe in.

Citizen: In America, we can decide about our own government.

Citizen: In America, we *are* the government! (*Everyone cheers.*)

Newscaster: Well, there you have it. That's what the citizens of America have to say! Today is July 4, 1776. Tune in next time, and we'll see how the rest of the story comes out. For now, this is [Newscaster's name] saying good-bye from Philadelphia.

Everyone: (*waving*) Good-bye!

The End